What a fly!

You gonna finish that?

BURP

BIG-TIME BUG!

SMARTEST PET

AMAZZZING!

BUZZ!

BEST FRIENDZZZ!

WUZZZUP!

Don't BUG me!

You're **so** fly!

Just wing it!

HEROZZZ!

📖 SCH

I SPY FLY GUY!

Tedd Arnold

Cartwheel BOOKS®

SCHOLASTIC INC.
New York   Toronto   London   Auckland
Sydney   Mexico City   New Delhi   Hong Kong

For Caleb, Aidan, Kellan, Ethan,
and Quinn—all cool guys!
—T.A.

All rights reserved. Published by Scholastic Inc. SCHOLASTIC, CARTWHEEL BOOKS,
and associated logos are trademarks and/or registered trademarks of Scholastic Inc.

Library of Congress Cataloging-in-Publication Data is available.

ISBN 978-0-545-11028-0

10 9 8 7 6 5 4 3 2 1   11 12 13 14 15 16 17/0

Printed in Malaysia 108
First printing, September 2009

A boy had a pet fly.
He named him Fly Guy.
Fly Guy could say
the boy's name—

BUZZ!

Chapter 1

One day, Buzz and
Fly Guy went outside.

"Let's play hide-and-seek," said Buzz.

Fly Guy hid
in the garbage can.
He always hid
in the garbage can.

He liked to eat while
Buzz looked for him.

"I spy Fly Guy!" said Buzz.
"It's my turn to hide."

6

Buzz hid in the garden shed
and shut the door.

Fly Guy found a way in.

"You are GOOD!" said Buzz.
"It's your turn to hide again."

Fly Guy hid in
the garbage can again.

Just then, the
garbageman came.

He dumped the garbage
into the truck and drove away.

Chapter 2

Buzz's dad was going
to work.

"Follow that truck!"
cried Buzz.

The truck drove and drove
and drove, all the way
to the town dump.

Buzz ran into the dump.
"Fly Guy, where are you?"

"Fly Guy," he cried.
"Answer me!"

A zillion flies all answered,

BUZZZZ

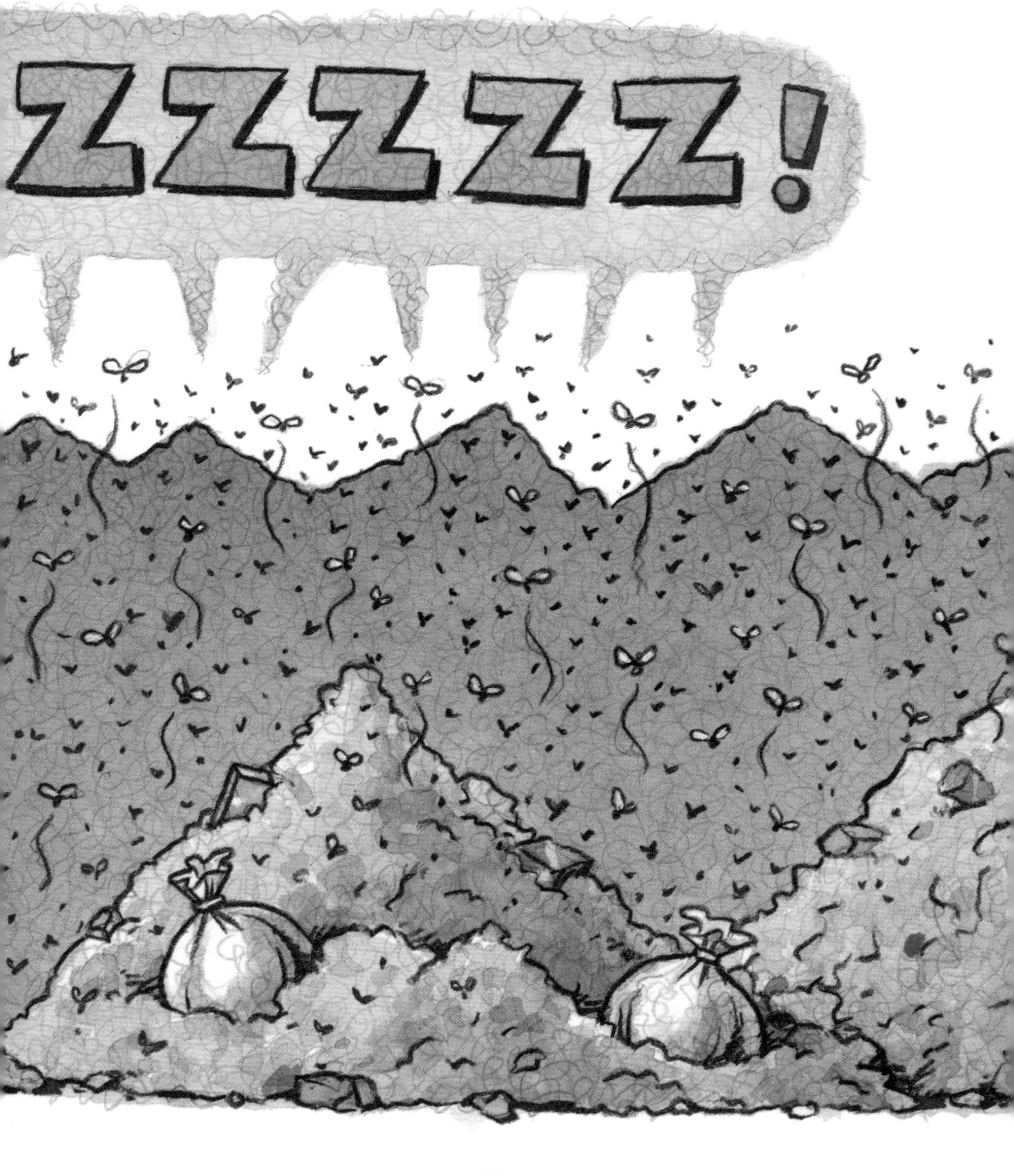
ZZZZZ!

"Oh, no!" cried Buzz.
"They all can say my name!
How will I find Fly Guy?"

Buzz spied a fly hiding.
"Do I spy Fly Guy?"
The fly flew away.

Buzz spied a fly eating.
"Do I spy Fly Guy?"
The fly boinked him
on the nose and flew away.

Buzz spied a fly landing
on his hand.
"Do I spy Fly Guy?"
The fly bit him and flew away.

Chapter 3

Buzz was sad.

Was Fly Guy gone forever?

He kicked a can.
He kicked a jar.

Then Buzz remembered.
They were still playing a game.

"Okay, Fly Guy," yelled Buzz,
"I give up. You win."

He heard a voice from above.

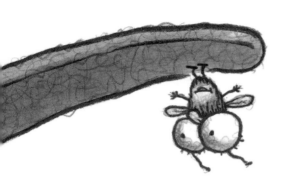

"I SPY FLY GUY!"
cried Buzz.

And Fly Guy said,

FLY GUY MEETS FLY GIRL!

Tedd Arnold

Cartwheel
B·O·O·K·S ®

SCHOLASTIC INC.
New York   Toronto   London   Auckland
Sydney   Mexico City   New Delhi   Hong Kong

For Elizabeth (Lizzz!) and Cortney
—T.A.

All rights reserved. Published by Scholastic Inc.
SCHOLASTIC, CARTWHEEL BOOKS, and associated logos
are trademarks and/or registered trademarks of Scholastic Inc.

Library of Congress Cataloging-in-Publication Data is available.

Arnold, Tedd.
Fly Guy meets Fly Girl / by Tedd Arnold.
p. cm.
Summary: When Fly Guy meets Fly Girl, he is amazed and smitten.
ISBN 978-0-545-11029-7
[1. Flies--Fiction.] I. Title.
PZ7.A7379Fl 2010   [E]--dc22
2009014182

ISBN: 978-0-545-11029-7

10 9 8 7 6 5 4 3 2 1   10 11 12 13 14/0

Printed in Malaysia 108
First printing, January 2010

A boy had a pet fly.
He named him Fly Guy.
Fly Guy could say
the boy's name—

BUZZ!

Chapter 1

One day, Buzz and
Fly Guy were bored.
Fly Guy said,

FUNZZIE?

"Yeah," said Buzz.
"Let's do something fun."

Buzz and Fly Guy
went for a walk.

They played chase.

They cooled off
in the fountain.

A girl was running.
A fly was chasing her.

"Don't worry," said Buzz.
"Flies aren't pests.
They are pets."

"I know," said the girl.
"This is my pet.
Her name is Fly Girl."

Chapter 2

Buzz said, "This is Fly Guy. He can do tricks."

"Fly Girl can do tricks, too!"
said the girl.

"Fly Guy eats gross stuff,"
said Buzz.

"Fly Girl eats grosser stuff!"
said the girl.

"Fly Guy can say my name," said Buzz.

"Fly Girl can say my name, too!"
said the girl.

"Do you want to play
on the swings?" said Buzz.
"Sure," said Liz.

Chapter 3

Fly Guy and Fly Girl
sat side by side.

Fly Guy said,

WUZZLE
WUZZLE

That is fly talk for
"You are nice."

Fly Girl said,

That is fly talk for
"You are nice, too."

Fly Guy and Fly Girl
talked and talked.

WUZZLE
WUZZLE

WUZZLE
WUZZY

WUZZY
WUZZLE

WUZZA
WUZZLE

WUZZLE
WUZZLE

WUZZY
WUZZA

Then Fly Guy said,

And Fly Girl said,

LIZZZ?

Fly Guy and Fly Girl both said,

WUZZLE WUZZZUP!

That is fly talk for
"Let's be friends."

"See you soon,"
said Buzz and Liz.

"Yeah," said Buzz.
"That was fun!"

BUZZ BOY AND FLY GUY

Tedd Arnold

Cartwheel
B·O·O·K·S ®

SCHOLASTIC INC.
New York   Toronto   London   Auckland
Sydney   Mexico City   New Delhi   Hong Kong

For Marcus—stay inspired!
—T.A.

Copyright © 2010 by Tedd Arnold.

All rights reserved. Published by Scholastic Inc. SCHOLASTIC, CARTWHEEL BOOKS,
and associated logos are trademarks and/or registered trademarks of Scholastic Inc.

No part of this publication may be reproduced, stored in a retrieval system, or transmitted
in any form or by any means, electronic, mechanical, photocopying, recording, or otherwise,
without written permission of the publisher. For information regarding permission,
write to Scholastic Inc., Attention: Permissions Department, 557 Broadway, New York, NY 10012.

Library of Congress Cataloging-in-Publication Data
Arnold, Tedd.
Buzz Boy and Fly Guy / by Tedd Arnold.
p. cm.
Summary: Buzz creates a comic book that features Buzz Boy and Fly Guy as the superheroes.
ISBN 0-545-22274-5
[1. Flies--Fiction. 2. Cartoons and comics--Fiction. 3. Superheroes--Fiction.] I. Title.
PZ7.A7379Bu 2010 [E]--dc22
2009038925

ISBN 978-0-545-22274-7

10 9 8 7 6 5 4 3 2 1   10 11 12 13 14

Printed in Malaysia 108
First printing, September 2010

A boy had a pet fly
named Fly Guy.
Fly Guy could say
the boy's name—

One night Buzz said,
"I made a book.
We are the superheroes."

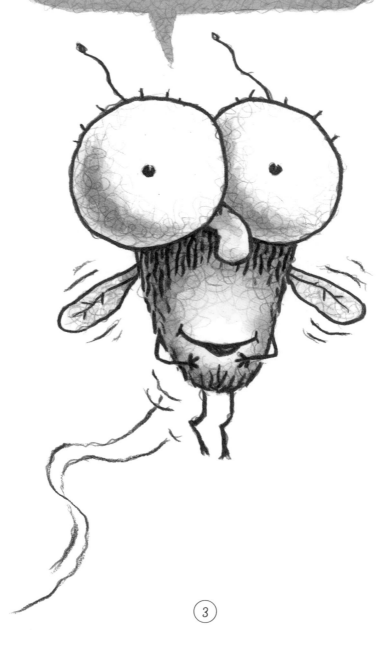

"Yes," said Buzz.
"I'll read it to you."

"THE AMAZING ADVENTURES OF BUZZ BOY AND FLY GUY"

BY ME (BUZZ)

ONE DAY BUZZ BOY
WOKE UP.

HE WAS THE SAME
SIZE AS FLY GUY!

BUZZ BOY LOOKED OUT THE WINDOW.

HE SAW A SLEEPING DRAGON.

CHAPTER TWO

THE DRAGON WAS STILL ASLEEP.

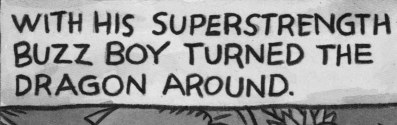

WITH HIS SUPERSTRENGTH BUZZ BOY TURNED THE DRAGON AROUND.

FLY GUY USED HIS SUPERLOUDNESS.

BUZZZZZZZ

THE DRAGON WOKE UP AND SHOT FIRE OUTSIDE.

THE PIRATE GUARDS
RAN AWAY.

CHAPTER THREE

BUZZ BOY AND FLY GUY WERE PUT IN JAIL ON THE PIRATE SHIP.

BUZZ BOY AND FLY GUY FLEW BACK TO THE ISLAND.

THEY MADE FRIENDS WITH THE DRAGON.

THE DRAGON TOOK THEIR HOUSE BACK HOME.

"The end," said Buzz.
Fly Guy said,

HEROZZZ!

"Superheroes," said Buzz.
"Want to read it again?"

FLY GUY VS. THE FLYSWATTER!

Tedd Arnold

SCHOLASTIC INC.

New York   Toronto   London   Auckland
Sydney   Mexico City   New Delhi   Hong Kong

For Brianna!

Copyright © 2011 by Tedd Arnold.

All rights reserved. Published by Scholastic Inc. SCHOLASTIC, CARTWHEEL BOOKS,
and associated logos are trademarks and/or registered trademarks of Scholastic Inc.

Library of Congress Cataloging-in-Publication Data

Arnold, Tedd.
Fly Guy vs. the fly swatter / Tedd Arnold. -- 1st ed.
p. cm.
Summary: Fly Guy unintentionally joins Buzz at school, and then goes
with his class on a field trip to a fly swatter factory.
ISBN 978-0-545-31286-8
[1. Flies--Fiction. 2. School field trips--Fiction.] I. Title. II.
Title: Fly Guy versus the fly swatter.
PZ7.A7379Fmv 2011
[E]--dc22

2010031381

ISBN 978-0-545-31286-8

10 9 8 7 6 5 4 3 2 1   11 12 13 14 15 16/0

Printed in Malaysia 108
First edition, August 2011

A boy had a pet fly.
He named him Fly Guy.
And Fly Guy could
say the boy's name—

BUZZ!

Chapter 1

One day, Fly Guy was eating breakfast in Buzz's backpack.

Buzz grabbed his backpack
and went to school.

At school, Fly Guy
flew out.

Then the teacher said,
"We are going on a field trip
to tour a factory."

Buzz said, "Fly Guy, you can ride in my pocket."

The class rode the bus to the factory.

They arrived at the factory.

Chapter 2

A tour guide led the
class inside.

Buzz said, "Fly Guy,
stay down in my pocket!"

The tour guide said,
"Here is our flyswatter
museum."

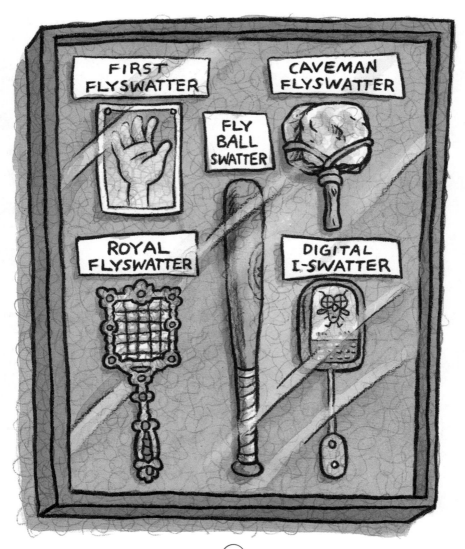

"Here is where we make the flyswatters," she said. "You may each have one."

"Now," said the guide, "here is
Fred the Fly to tell you more!"

Fly Guy peeked out.

"Boys and girls," said Fred.
"We know flies play in slime."
Fly Guy nodded.

"Flies eat garbage!"
Fly Guy smiled.

"Flies are nasty!"
Fly Guy got mad.

"That's why, boys and girls,"
Fred the Fly shouted,
"we need . . .

the flyswatter of the future—
the **Super Swatter 6000!**"

Chapter 3

"Now let's see what the Super Swatter can do!" said Fred. "Bring out the fly!"

The tour guide brought
out a tiny fly in a jar.

"Release the fly!"
yelled Fred.

The Super Swatter
started swatting.

Fly Guy cried,

Fly Guy flew to the little fly.

The Super Swatter kept swatting.

Fly Guy took the fly
to an open window.

The Super Swatter kept swatting.

Fly Guy flew past
Fred the Fly.

WHAP

WHAP

WHAP

WHAP

WHAP

WHAP

WHAP

WHAP

The Super Swatter kept swatting.

Fly Guy flew past the
flyswatter machines.
The Super Swatter kept swatting.

"Stop! Stop!" yelled Fred.
"Everyone out! No more
factory tours, ever!"

Back at school, the class made an art project. Everyone agreed—

BEST FIELD TRIP EVER!

RIDE, FLY GUY, RIDE!

Tedd Arnold

Cartwheel BOOKS®

SCHOLASTIC INC.
New York   Toronto   London   Auckland
Sydney   Mexico City   New Delhi   Hong Kong

Ride, Garrett, ride!

Library of Congress Cataloging-in-Publication Data is available.

ISBN 978-0-545-22276-1

10 9 8 7 6 5 4 3 2 1   12 13 14 15 16 17/0

Printed in Malaysia 108
First edition, January 2012

A boy had a pet fly.
He named him Fly Guy.
And Fly Guy could
say the boy's name—

BUZZ!

Chapter 1

One day, Dad said, "Who wants to go for a ride?"

"We do!" said Buzz and
Fly Guy.

"Everyone buckle up!" Dad said. Then they hit the road with the windows down.

Buzz said, "Oops, Fly Guy, you need some air!"

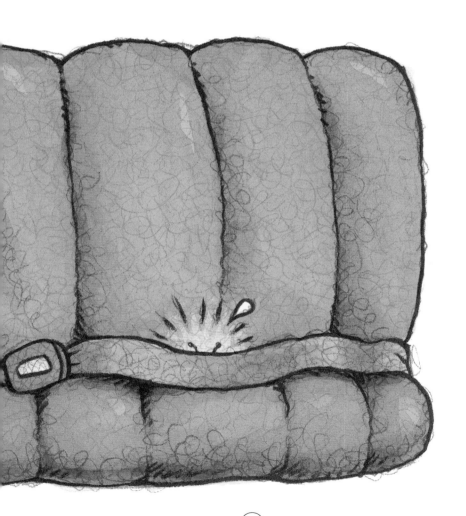

Buzz stuck his hand out the window and pretended it was an airplane.

Suddenly, wind blew in the car and carried Fly Guy out of the window . . .

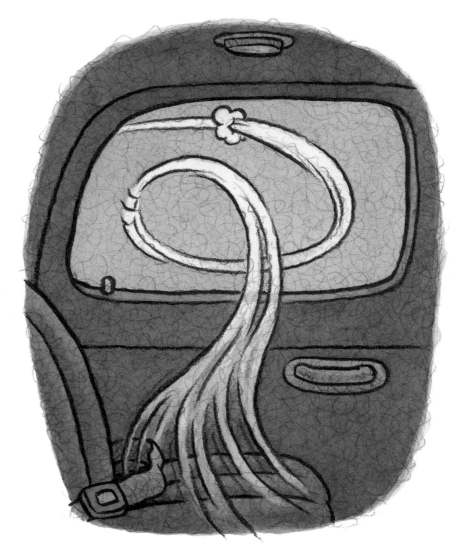

. . . and into a passing truck.

Chapter 2

"Follow that truck!"

cried Buzz.

Meanwhile, in the truck,
Fly Guy tumbled into
the truck driver's mouth.

PTOOIE!

The truck driver spit Fly Guy
out the window . . .

. . . and into a passing
motorboat.

"Follow that boat!" cried Buzz.

Meanwhile, on the boat, Fly
Guy saw a man put a bug on
a big hook.

Fly Guy jumped overboard . . .

. . . and onto a passing circus train.

"Follow that train!" cried Buzz.

Meanwhile, on the train,
Fly Guy surprised a sleepy
elephant.

The elephant blew him off
the train . . .

. . . and onto an airplane.

"Follow that airplane!"
cried Buzz.

Meanwhile, on the airplane,
the pilot saw Fly Guy and
turned on the wipers.

"Follow that . . . I mean,
follow Fly Guy!" cried Buzz.

Just then,
a rocket
roared up
from the
ground.

Chapter 3

"Follow that rocket!" cried Buzz.

Buzz and Dad landed. The rocket
raced into space. "Will Fly Guy
survive?" asked Buzz.

"Fly Guy, you're here!" cried
Buzz. "The rocket didn't
take you to space!"

Dad said, "Let's ride home."
And Fly Guy said—

MORE RIDEZZZ!

THERE'S A FLY GUY IN MY SOUP

Tedd Arnold

Cartwheel Books • New York

An Imprint of Scholastic Inc.

Specially for the Beecher Doll Club
and everyone at the Arnot Art Museum

All rights reserved. Published by Scholastic Inc. SCHOLASTIC, CARTWHEEL BOOKS,
and associated logos are trademarks and/or registered trademarks of Scholastic Inc.

Library of Congress Cataloging-in-Publication Data

Arnold, Tedd.
There's a Fly Guy in my soup / Tedd Arnold.
p. cm. -- (Fly Guy ; 12)
Summary: When Fly Guy is not allowed in the restaurant with Buzz's
family he follows his nose and ends up in the soup.
ISBN 978-0-545-31284-4
1. Restaurants--Juvenile fiction. 2. Flies--Juvenile fiction. [1.
Restaurants--Fiction. 2. Flies--Fiction.] I. Title. II. Title: There is
a Fly Guy in my soup. III. Series: Arnold, Tedd. Fly Guy ; #12.

PZ7.A7379Thm 2012
[E]--dc23

2012000801

ISBN 978-0-545-31284-4

10 9 8 7 6 5 4 3 2 1   12 13 14 15 16 17

Printed in Malaysia 108

First edition, September 2012

A boy had a pet fly.
He named him Fly Guy.
And Fly Guy could
say the boy's name—

BUZZ!

Chapter 1

One day, Fly Guy went with Buzz, Mom, and Dad on a long trip.

They drove until dinnertime.
They stopped at a hotel.
"Yay!" said Buzz. "I love hotels!"

"Cool room," said Buzz.
"Time for dinner," said Dad.
"There is a nice restaurant downstairs," said Mom,
"but Fly Guy can't go there."

"Fly Guy can eat outside," said Buzz. "Right, Fly Guy?"

Fly Guy flew outside.

He found a
trash can.

He found
a puddle.

He found a sticky spot.

He found the biggest, slimiest
garbage can ever.

But he didn't
find anything that
he wanted to eat.

Chapter 2

Then Fly Guy smelled
something wonderful.

Fly Guy followed
the smell.

At last, he found where he wanted to eat!

Fly Guy needed to wash
before dinner.

He spied a small round
bathtub with warm
brown water. Perfect!

Fly Guy jumped in.

He washed his face and hands.

He washed his armpits.

He washed between his toes.

Chapter 3

Fly Guy's bathtub was picked up and carried to another room.

It was set down on a table
in front of a lady.

The lady screamed, "Waiter! There's a fly in my soup!"

The lady jumped up. Her soup and Fly Guy went flying...

...into another lady's soup.

That lady jumped up. Her soup
and the first lady's soup
and Fly Guy went flying...

...onto a gentleman's head.

The gentleman jumped up.
The soup and Fly Guy
and the gentleman's hair
went flying....

Everyone jumped up. Everyone's soup and Fly Guy and the gentleman's hair went flying.

Fly Guy still needed a bath.
Buzz, Mom, and Dad
needed a bath.

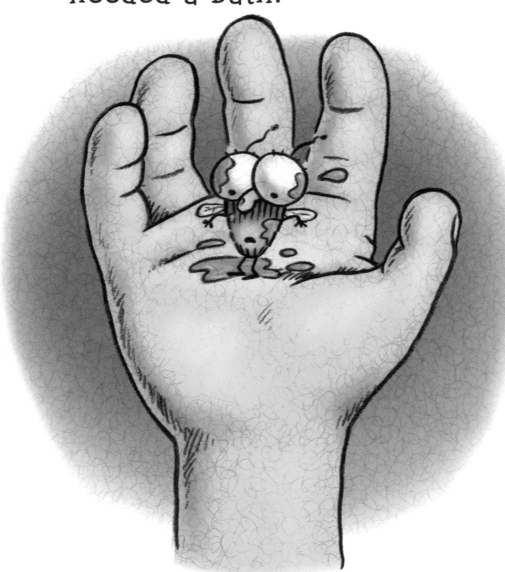

Everyone needed a bath.
"Last one in the pool is a
rotten egg!" yelled Buzz.

FLY GUY
is all the buzzzzz!

A Theodor Seuss Geisel Honor Book

Tedd Arnold

SUPER FLY GUY
Tedd Arnold

SHOO, FLY GUY!
Tedd Arnold

THERE WAS AN OLD LADY WHO SWALLOWED FLY GUY
Tedd Arnold

FLY HIGH, FLY GUY!
Tedd Arnold

HOORAY FOR FLY GUY!
Tedd Arnold

A Theodor Seuss Geisel Honor Book
I SPY FLY GUY!
Tedd Arnold

FLY GUY MEETS FLY GIRL!
Tedd Arnold

BUZZ BOY AND FLY GUY
Tedd Arnold

FLY GUY VS. THE FLYSWATTER!
Tedd Arnold

RIDE, FLY GUY, RIDE!
Tedd Arnold

NEW YORK TIMES BESTSELLING SERIES
THERE'S A FLY GUY IN MY SOUP
Tedd Arnold

NEW YORK TIMES BESTSELLING SERIES
FLY GUY AND THE FRANKENFLY
Tedd Arnold

NEW YORK TIMES BESTSELLING SERIES
FLY GUY'S AMAZING TRICKS
Tedd Arnold

For more Fly Guy fun, visit scholastic.com/flyguy

■ SCHOLASTIC

FLYGUY14   cartwheel books